Lost in
Las Vegas

For Judith and Zack. The truth is out there.
—D.G.

Lost in Las Vegas

by Dan Greenburg

illustrated by Macky Pamintuan

A STEPPING STONE BOOK™

Random House 🏠 New York

Copyright © 2006 by Dan Greenburg
Illustrations copyright © 2006 by Macky Pamintuan

All rights reserved.
Published in the United States by Random House Children's Books,
a division of Random House, Inc., New York.

RANDOM HOUSE and colophon are registered trademarks and
A STEPPING STONE BOOK and colophon are trademarks of
Random House, Inc.

www.steppingstonesbooks.com
www.randomhouse.com/kids

Educators and librarians, for a variety of teaching tools, visit us at
www.randomhouse.com/teachers

Library of Congress Cataloging-in-Publication Data
Greenburg, Dan.
Lost in Las Vegas / by Dan Greenburg ; illustrated by Macky Pamintuan.
p.   cm. — (Weird planet ; 2)
"A Stepping Stone Book."
SUMMARY: After crashing their spaceship in the Nevada desert, Klatu, Lek, and
their sister Ploo go to Las Vegas in search of the one mechanic who can fix it.
ISBN 0-375-83345-5 (pbk.) — ISBN 0-375-93345-X (lib. bdg.)
[1. Extraterrestrial beings—Fiction. 2. Brothers and sisters—Fiction. 3. Las
Vegas (Nev.)—Fiction. 4. Science fiction. 5. Humorous stories.]
I. Pamintuan, Macky, ill. II. Title.
PZ7.G8278Los 2006
[Fic]—dc22   2005044729

Printed in the United States of America
10 9 8 7 6 5 4 3 2 1
First Edition

Contents

Desperately Seeking Jo-Jo

"Push the pedal, Lek!" Klatu shouted.

"I *am* pushing the pedal, you *varna*!" Lek shouted back.

Klatu was kneeling on the seat of the slow-moving station wagon. His long, gray Looglish fingers were wrapped around the steering wheel.

Lek was lying on the floor of the car, just below Klatu. He'd pushed the gas pedal down as far as it would go, but the car acted like it was sick. It jerked. It sputtered. It coughed. It slowly rolled to a stop.

"It must be out of energy cells," said Lek.

"Woof!" said the puppy in the backseat.

The puppy was Ploo, their little sister. Ploo didn't usually look like a puppy. Usually she looked just like *they* did. But Ploo got captured by soldiers from the Area 51 army base. Her new friend, Lily, helped her escape. Ploo had to morph into doggy shape to hide from Lily's scary father, Major Paine. He was the boss of the army base, and he was trying hard to recapture her.

This was all Klatu's fault, of course. He was the one who'd talked them into flying to planet Earth to do extra-credit science projects for school. He was also the one who'd crash-landed their spacecraft and nearly gotten them killed.

Klatu, Lek, and Ploo got out of the car. They had been traveling all night. A full moon cast eerie blue-white light on the Nevada desert sand dunes. Deadly snakes and scorpions hid in the shadows, waiting for victims to walk by.

"Look!" cried Lek. "See those bright lights ahead of us?"

In the middle of the ghostly desert were buildings, glaring lights, beeping horns, and traffic jams.

"That must be Las Vegas, the Earth city that Lily told us about," said Lek.

"I have heard of this Las Vegas," said Klatu. "It is where people come to gum-ball."

"You mean *gamble*?" said Lek.

"That is what I said, *gamble*," Klatu answered. "I used to know what that word meant, but it fell out of my head when we cra— when we landed."

"I do not know what it means, either," said Lek. "Ploo, do you know what *gamble* means?"

They didn't understand woofs, so Ploo spoke directly to their minds by E.S.P.

No, Lek. But here is what I do know, she esped. *I know that we must go to Las Vegas and find a woman named Jo-Jo. Lily says she is the one human who can fix our spacecraft. Unless we find Jo-Jo, we will never get off this stupid planet. And we will never see our dear planet Loogl again.*

They left the car and began walking in the direction of the lights. A chilly desert wind made them shiver.

Uh-oh, Ploo esped.

"What is wrong, Ploo?"

I am starting to morph. I am morphing into my Looglish shape again. Owww! Owww!

Ploo's doggy shape grew soft and

mushy. Then it pushed and pulled and smooshed into something entirely different. A beautiful little three-foot-tall alien girl with big black eyes, gray skin, and a single antenna growing out of her head.

Bright Lights, Big City

The closer Lek, Ploo, and Klatu got to Las Vegas, the brighter and the noisier it became. Then the city swallowed them up. They walked around a corner and came face to face with a monster.

"Hide!" shrieked Klatu, and ducked behind a car.

The monster was huge and round. It was covered with tubes of different-colored lights. The lighted tubes were turning off and on in speedy patterns. They seemed to be moving in an angry way. What kind of monster could it be?

Klatu figured he'd better send peaceful thoughts to the monster's mind.

We come in peace, Klatu esped in the monster's direction. *We hope you come in peace.*

"Klatu, I do not think that thing is alive," said Ploo in her own tiny voice. "I think it is what humans call a neon sign. See how it is covered with words?"

The sign said DRIVE-THROUGH WEDDING CHAPEL. OPEN 24 HOURS.

"Well, it seems alive to *me*," said Klatu. "Also angry."

Ahead of them now, on both sides of the street, were huge hotels with strange things going on in front of them. Like a volcano with flames shooting thirty feet into the air.

"That small mountain is on fire!" cried Klatu.

"But nobody seems upset," said Ploo. "Perhaps such things are normal here."

In front of another hotel was a pirate ship. Two bands of pirates fought each other on the deck of the ship. The ship was on fire!

"There is another fire!" cried Klatu.

"Nobody seems upset by that one, either," said Ploo.

One hotel was built in the shape of a giant glass pyramid. Another hotel was in the shape of an enormous sinking ship. In front of some hotels were amazing neon signs, waterfalls, and more things on fire.

"This is a strange, strange place," said Ploo. "Even stranger than Mordoonk."

"Look." Klatu pointed across the street. "The Awful Tower!"

Ploo and Lek looked.

"You mean the *Eiffel* Tower?" said Lek. "The famous tower in Paris? I did not think that Paris was in Nevada. I thought it was in France."

"And over there," said Klatu. "The Umpire State Building!"

"The *Empire* State Building?" said Lek. "That is in New York City. I did not think that New York City was in Nevada, either."

"They not only have whole cities here," said Klatu, impressed. "They have entire *planets*."

Klatu pointed across the highway. A neon sign flashed the words PLANET HOLLYWOOD.

"Planet Hollywood must be a very small planet," said Lek. "Smaller than the one humans call Mercury."

The back end of a large car was sticking out of the wall of Planet Hollywood, right above the doorway.

"How did a car crash into a building so high up?" asked Klatu.

"Humans must be really awful drivers,"

said Lek. "Even worse than Klatu."

"Hey!" said Klatu. "I am a *great* driver!"

"This is a very dangerous place," said Ploo. "We must be careful here. And we must find Jo-Jo as soon as possible."

"But we do not even know where to look for her," said Lek. "We will never find her. Without Jo-Jo, we are finished! We are doomed!"

Klatu ignored him. Ploo rolled her eyes. Lek worried way too much.

"What is that over there?" asked Klatu. "The thing that looks like a sinking ship?"

"It says Titanic Hotel," said Ploo.

"I like how it looks," said Klatu. "Let us go there first to look for Jo-Jo."

"We should morph into human shape first," said Lek.

"Yes. And one of us should look like an *older* human," said Ploo.

"Older humans have gray noses," said Klatu. "I shall grow a gray nose."

"Older humans have gray *beards*," Lek corrected. "Not noses."

"That is what I *said*," Klatu answered grumpily. "All right, time to morph. Ready, little brother? Ready, little sister? One . . . two . . . three . . . morph!"

With a soft sound, the three alien kids grew upward and outward. Their arms and legs got thicker. Their heads got smaller. Their eyes shrank down to the beady little things that humans had.

The kids had chosen haircuts and clothes they'd seen in their textbooks about planet Earth. But their textbooks were very old. They'd picked old-fashioned sailor suits. Button-up shoes. Straw hats with ribbons. Klatu had a long gray beard.

Their human forms wouldn't last more

than an *arp*. They set the *arp*-timers on their wrists. One *arp* of Loogl time was about the same as one hour of Earth time. There were fifty *mynts* in an *arp*. Fifty *mynts* till they started looking like aliens again.

"And now," said Lek, "we need to speak their language. Here is English gum for everybody."

He handed green gum balls to Klatu and to Ploo. Then he popped one into his own mouth and began to chew. The flavor would also last about an *arp*. When it faded, they would hardly be able to speak English at all.

Klatu, Lek, and Ploo walked into the Titanic Hotel. The hotel had been built to look like a famous ship that sank in the Atlantic Ocean. All the floors in the hotel were tilted. The lowest corner of every room was partly underwater.

They walked up to the tilted front desk. Behind the desk was a clerk dressed in a navy blue ship-officer's uniform.

"Welcome aboard, mates," said the clerk.

"Do you know somebody named Jo-Jo?" Ploo asked the clerk.

"No," said the clerk. "Would you folks like to rent a room here?"

"What would it cost?" asked Klatu.

"Three hundred a night," said the clerk.

"Three hundred *what*?" asked Lek.

"Dollars," said the clerk.

"Ha," said Lek. He didn't know if three hundred dollars was a lot or a little.

"But we do have better rates for gamblers," said the clerk.

"Better means higher?" asked Klatu.

"Better means lower," said the clerk. "But that's only for big gamblers."

"Well, *we* are big gamblers," said Klatu. "Very big. The biggest."

"How much do you usually bet when you gamble?" asked the clerk.

Klatu looked at Lek and Ploo. He was hoping they would esp him a number. They didn't. "How much would be very big?" asked Klatu.

"A thousand dollars a bet," said the clerk.

"What a coincidence," said Klatu. "That is exactly what we usually bet."

The clerk was impressed. He walked over to another man and whispered in his ear. The other man nodded. He had medals on his chest and looked important. He was the manager of the hotel.

"We're going to give you a complimentary room," said the clerk.

"*Complimentary* means the room will

say nice things about us?" Klatu asked.

"*Complimentary* means the room is free," said the manager.

"Good," said Klatu. He thought *free* meant the room was not being used by anybody else.

"You're sure you're big gamblers, though? High rollers?" said the manager.

On planet Loogl, one of Klatu's favorite sports was strapping himself to a huge stone wheel and rolling down a hill.

"Back home I am a very high roller," said Klatu.

A bellboy in a shipmate's uniform took them up to their room. It had enormous beds and a marble floor. It had round portholes instead of windows. The floor was tilted. The lowest end had been made into a marble bathtub. It had shiny brass handles and faucets. Fluffy towels and a bar of soap were piled next to it.

"Can I take you to the casino now?" asked the bellboy.

"Why not?" said Klatu. Klatu, Lek, and Ploo lined up. They followed the bellboy out the door. They marched down the hall behind him. Lek tapped the bellboy on the shoulder.

"We are desperately looking for somebody named Jo-Jo," said Lek. "Do you know anyone by that name?"

"Why are you desperate to find Jo-Jo?" asked the bellboy.

Lek wondered if the word *desperately* had been a mistake. "It is not because she knows how to fix spaceships," he said.

Lek, you varna! esped Klatu. *We do not want anyone to know we have a spaceship!*

"We have no spaceship," said Lek

quickly. "Why would we? Even if we had, would it be broken? No! So why would we need Jo-Jo to fix it? A foolish thought. Ha ha!"

Enough, Lek! esped Ploo.

Be quiet! esped Klatu.

"A guy named Joe works on the roulette wheel," said the bellboy. "Maybe he's the person you're looking for."

Lek, Ploo, and Klatu were thrilled. Humans who worked on wheels were called mechanics. Jo-Jo was a mechanic. So the person working on the wheel was Jo-Jo!

The bellboy thought for *sure* that telling these weirdos about the person who ran the roulette wheel would earn him a tip. He was wrong.

Gum-balling

The bellboy stopped at the casino floor and pointed across the room. "The roulette wheel is over there," he said.

"Many thanks," said Ploo.

Klatu, Lek, and Ploo walked through the casino. It was a very large room. The carpet on the floor had swirly patterns in browns and greens. It looked like somebody had thrown up on it. Probably somebody had. The room was bright, but there were no windows. It was impossible to tell if it was night or day.

They passed hundreds of slot machines. Each machine had a slot to drop

coins into. Each machine had a long handle on its side. Each machine had three dials on it. People stood in front of the machines and dropped coins into the slots. They pulled the handles and watched the dials on the machines spin.

The casino was filled with the *ding-ding-ding* and the *dong-dong-dong* of thousands of coins being dropped into the slot machines.

"I read about this in Earthling Studies," said Klatu. "See those machines? Trash cans. When humans have money they no longer want, they put it in these trash cans. They pull the levers to flush the money down."

A little old lady wearing a baseball cap hit a jackpot. Quarters came gushing out of her machine. She squealed in surprise.

"What just happened?" asked Ploo.

"Sometimes the trash cans get clogged and they back up," Klatu explained. "Then the money comes back out."

The little old lady scooped all the coins out of the machine. She put them into a big plastic cup. Then she began dropping coins back into the slot machine.

"See?" said Klatu. "The poor human has to put every coin back into the trash can until they are gone again."

They finally got to the roulette wheel. The man in charge wore a loose tuxedo and a tight smile.

"Good morning," said the man.

"Good riddance," said Klatu. "Do you know how to fix spaceships?"

The man thought this might be a trick question. "Who wants to know?" he said.

"Are you Jo-Jo?" asked Klatu.

"No, just Joe," said the man. He

smelled a little like perfume and a little like sweat.

"Do you know anybody named Jo-Jo?" asked Lek.

"Maybe," said Joe. "Play roulette while I think about it."

He does not know anyone named Jo-Jo, esped Lek. *We will never find Jo-Jo!*

"How do you play roulette?" asked Ploo.

"You see this wheel?" said Joe.

There was a large wooden wheel resting on the table. Inside the wheel was a groove with little pockets in it. There were numbers painted in all the pockets.

"Now watch this," said Joe.

He spun the wheel. Then he dropped a little wooden ball into the groove. The ball went racing around and around. When the wheel stopped spinning, the ball dropped into a pocket with a little clicking sound. In the pocket was the number seven.

"Lucky number seven," said Joe. "If you had bet on number seven, you'd have won a lot of money."

In the ceiling above the roulette wheel was a tiny TV camera. In a room above the casino was a short, heavy man. He was wearing a white dinner jacket with a purple rose in the lapel and smoking a stinky, fat cigar. He was Armand, the casino boss.

Armand was watching the roulette wheel on a small black-and-white TV screen. "The crazy-looking people we put in the Captain's Suite are going to play roulette," said Armand. "The old man, the boy, and the little girl."

"Let's see if they're really high rollers," said a tall, skinny guy in a shiny black suit. His name was Marcel. Under his long,

crooked nose, Marcel had a mustache that looked like a caterpillar.

Back at the roulette wheel, Joe asked, "Would you like to place a bet?"

"Yes, please," said Ploo.

"Not *you*, little lady," said Joe. "Children aren't allowed to gamble. Only old guys like Grandpa here." He winked at Klatu. "How much would you like to bet, sir?"

Klatu handed Joe a platinum coin from Loogl. Joe studied the coin. He knew coins very well. He knew platinum when he saw it. He knew that platinum was worth lots more than either gold or silver.

"Okay," said Joe. "What number do you think the ball will stop on?"

Klatu looked at Ploo. *Can you help me here, Ploo?* esped Klatu.

Ploo liked when her big brother asked for her help. It didn't happen often. Mostly he needed her to play mind games. Ploo was very good at mind games. She could cast her thoughts out like a fishing net. When she pulled her thought net back in again, marvelous things would be caught inside of it. Things from people's minds. Or things that hadn't even happened yet.

Tell me how beautiful I am, Ploo esped.

Do we have to do this every single time? esped Klatu.

Every single time, esped Ploo.

Ploo, you are the most beautiful little girl in the entire Darkside of Loogl, Klatu esped.

And what is the most beautiful thing about me? Ploo esped.

Your eyes, Ploo. Your eyes are bigger and blacker and . . . and . . . deeper than the Sea

28

of Nothingness, esped Klatu. All right?

Joe couldn't hear their conversation. To him, it looked like they were just standing there.

"Are you going to pick a number or aren't you?" Joe asked.

"I am *thinking*, I am *thinking*!" said Klatu. Well, Ploo? he esped.

Ploo closed her eyes, emptied her mind, and cast out her thought net. She pulled it back in and looked at what was flopping around in there. It was slippery. A human number. Kind of hard to see. It looked like two sticks close together. It looked like . . . What did humans call that number?

Ploo esped the number directly to Klatu's mind: Eleven.

"Eleven," Klatu told Joe.

Lek tried to think what the number

eleven looked like backward. It looked the same forward and backward. In his mind, he spelled it backward three times for luck: *nevele, nevele, nevele. This does not sound right,* he worried. *It will never work.*

Joe took Klatu's platinum coin and gave the wheel a spin. He dropped the little wooden ball. It raced around and around as the wheel spun. The wheel slowed down. The ball dropped into the pocket with number . . . eleven.

"Eleven!" said Joe.

"Is that good?" Klatu asked.

"For *you*, yes," said Joe.

Upstairs, Armand seemed quite pained. "They won!" he said. "Darn!"

"Don't worry, Boss. It won't happen again," said Marcel.

"What did we win?" Klatu asked Joe.

Joe handed him a heavy sack of

money. "Ten thousand dollars," he said. "Would you like to place another bet?"

Klatu looked at Ploo. She raised one eyebrow. She liked having human eyebrows. They were fun.

Um, okay, Ploo, your antenna is longer and wavier than a sea worm. All right? Klatu esped.

Good enough, Klatu, esped Ploo.

Ploo closed her eyes again. She cleared her mind and cast out her thought net. Another human number got tangled up in it. It looked like the number . . . three. She esped it to Klatu.

"Three," Klatu told Joe.

Joe spun the wheel again. He dropped the little wooden ball. The wheel slowed down. The ball came to rest on . . . three.

"Three," said Joe. His tight smile had faded. He seemed sad. He gave Klatu another heavy sack of money.

Watching this on the TV screen upstairs, Armand punched a wall. "I don't believe this! They won again!" he shouted.

"It's just luck, Boss," said Marcel.

"Would you like to bet again, sir?" Joe asked Klatu.

Klatu looked at Ploo. *Ploo, your hands are so soft and gray,* he esped. *Your fingers are graceful and . . . and . . .*

. . . *and?* esped Ploo.

. . . *and longer than my feet,* esped Klatu.

I do not care for the "longer than my feet" part, esped Ploo. *But the rest was okay.*

Ploo closed her eyes again and cleared her mind. She cast out her thought net again. She esped another number to her brother: *thirteen.*

"Thirteen," said Klatu.

"The gentleman's bet is lucky number thirteen," said Joe.

Joe spun the wheel and dropped the ball. It came to rest on . . . thirteen.

"Thirteen," said Joe. He did not sound happy at all.

"They won *again!*" shouted Armand upstairs. "That's three times in a row! We're out thirty thousand dollars, Marcel!"

"You think they're cheating on us, Boss?" asked Marcel.

"No, Marcel," said Armand, "I don't think they're cheating on us. I *know* they're cheating on us! I just can't figure out how they're doing it."

"Want me to rough them up a little, Boss?" asked Marcel.

"*More* than a little," said Armand. "But first, I want you to follow them. Stick to them like orange cat hair on a good black suit. I want to know everywhere they go. Everything they do. Everyone they talk to. You got that?"

"Right, Boss," said Marcel.

Ten feet below them, Joe handed Klatu a third heavy bag of money.

"The wheel is tired now," said Joe. "The wheel wants to rest."

Klatu, Lek, and Ploo nodded. That made sense to them.

$30,000 Is Heavy

Klatu, Lek, and Ploo walked back through the casino. Each carried a bag of money.

"This money is really heavy," said Klatu. "Do we have to carry it with us?"

"Joe seemed so sad when he gave it to us," said Ploo. "Maybe we should give it back to him."

"You might hurt his feelings," said Lek.

Klatu, Lek, and Ploo definitely didn't want to hurt Joe's feelings. They had read what humans do when you hurt their feelings.

They walked on.

"I am just a little girl," said Ploo. "I should not have to carry such a heavy bag."

"Then why do we not just leave the money here?" said Klatu. "We can pick it up after we find Jo-Jo."

"Good idea," said Lek. He put his bag of money down on the floor. Ploo and Klatu put their bags of money down beside Lek's. They walked away through the casino.

"Hey!" called a voice behind them. They turned around. A guard in a blue uniform was running after them, carrying the bags of money. "You folks forgot these!" he said. "You sure don't want to do that around here!"

Klatu, Lek, and Ploo picked up the heavy sacks. Ploo sighed. Money was a pain in the arm. When they passed the slot machines, she had an idea.

Why do we not throw some of our money into these trash cans? she esped.

Great idea, esped Lek. They started feeding coins into the slot machines. But then they hit a jackpot. Coins came gushing out

again. Now they'd have to take the extra ones with them, too.

"Darn," said Klatu. "More money! These trash cans are broken. We will have to throw this money out somewhere else."

They walked outside. Lek blinked in the sunlight. It was bright and hot. The hotel next door looked like a huge circus tent. A big sign out in front of the hotel said CIRCUS CIRCUS.

"Look!" shouted Lek. He started jumping up and down. Ploo and Klatu looked.

He was pointing to another sign. It said AT CIRCUS CIRCUS—SEE JOJO.

"This is almost too easy!" cried Lek.

They raced into Circus Circus. They were still carrying their bags of money.

A man followed them at a safe distance. He was wearing a black trench coat with the collar turned up to hide his face. Marcel.

Inside Circus Circus was another casino with hundreds of slot machines. Hundreds of people stood at the slot machines, dropping coins into them. It was a lot like the casino at the Titanic Hotel. Then the kids looked up.

High above the slot machines, acrobats swung back and forth on trapezes. They flew through the air and were caught by other acrobats. None of the people at the slot machines were watching the acrobats. They were only looking at the slot machines.

Lek did see one human looking up at the acrobats. It was a small boy standing next to him. The boy wore a striped T-shirt and short pants. His face looked sticky, and he smelled a little sour.

"Why are these humans flying through the air?" Lek asked the boy.

"If you swallow a booger, you'll die," said the boy.

"Really?" said Lek. "I did not know that." He felt this was an important fact about Earth. "Remember," he whispered to Ploo and Klatu. "If you swallow a booger, you'll die." Lek turned back to the boy. "What is a booger?"

"If you step on a crack, you'll die," said the boy.

"Thank you," said Lek. Collecting ways you could die happened to be a hobby of Lek's. Lek felt he owed the boy something in return. "I know a shortcut through space," he said. "Just go through the Gamma Wormhole and you'll avoid an entire galaxy."

"Worms taste yucky," said the boy. "If you eat a worm, you'll die."

"Hmm," said Lek. He added that to his memory, too.

At the far corner of the room was a fancy doorway covered with glittery gold paint. A very small human girl wandered away from her mother and toddled through the doorway. The boy who told Lek that swallowing boogers made you die followed the girl through the doorway.

Ploo noticed the sign above the doorway: THIS WAY TO JOJO.

"Look!" said Ploo.

Ploo, Lek, and Klatu raced through the doorway. It led into a much smaller room. In the room was a cage with black steel bars, and inside the cage was a huge white tiger with brown stripes. There was a strong smell of animal in the room. A sign on the cage said JOJO.

This was confusing. Could this stripy animal really know how to fix a broken space-craft? No. Ploo was pretty sure that Lily said Jo-Jo was a human, not a stripy animal.

Huge posters on the walls showed JoJo the tiger doing circus tricks. Standing on her hind legs. Jumping through a hoop of fire. Posing with Sigmund and Rolf, the famous Las Vegas magicians.

The woman in charge of JoJo's cage wore a sparkly white jumpsuit. She was standing off to the side of the room, talking on her cell phone.

The small human girl standing next to the cage squealed with happiness. "Tigger!" she said. She reached through the bars of the cage to pet JoJo, but her arm wasn't long enough. "Pet Tigger!" she said.

She stuck her shoulder through the bars and reached out again. Her arm still wasn't long enough to reach the tiger. She squeezed between the bars and into the tiger's cage.

The woman in the sparkly white jump-suit didn't see this. She was too busy talking on her phone. She wandered out of the room.

Ploo was shocked to see what the little human girl had done. She ran up to the tiger's cage.

Ploo, what are you doing? Lek esped.

Going into the cage to save the little human, Ploo esped.

Do not do that! Lek esped. *The stripy thing will eat you!*

Ploo squeezed between the bars of the tiger's cage. She grabbed the little girl and tried to push her back through the bars.

"No!" said the little girl, struggling. "Tigger! Pet Tigger!" She refused to let Ploo push her out of the cage.

Ploo, watch out! *esped Lek.* The stripy thing is coming!

Ploo turned around. Uh-oh! The stripy thing was padding heavily over to Ploo and the little girl. It looked a lot bigger and scarier now that she was inside the cage. Then Ploo had an idea.

I will morph into an animal with a long trunk and huge ears. Stripy things are afraid of animals with long trunks and huge ears. I read that in Earth Animal Studies.

It is too dangerous to morph into something bigger than you are! **Lek warned.**

You cannot morph from one shape to another! **esped Klatu.** *Not unless you wait one arp! Not unless you go back to your true shape first!*

Do not worry! **Ploo esped.** *I have done this dozens of times before!*

Ploo tried to morph—1 . . . 2 . . . 3 . . . but nothing happened . . . 4 . . . 5 . . . 6 . . .

still nothing . . . 7 . . . 8 . . . 9 . . . Her skin seemed tighter, but that was all. She still looked like a little human girl. Not like a big animal with a trunk, tusks, and huge ears.

The, uh, morphing does not seem to be going so well, Ploo esped.

I told you not to do this! esped Lek. Did I tell you not to do this?

The tiger began to growl.

Morph, Ploo, morph! Lek esped.

Please morph, Ploo! Klatu esped.

Ploo tried to send peaceful thoughts directly to the tiger's mind.

Do not eat little girls, she esped. *Little girls are nice to stripy things. Little girls would never eat a stripy thing. Stripy things would never eat a little girl.*

The tiger flattened its ears. It wrinkled its nose. It opened its terrible mouth and showed Ploo its terrible teeth. The teeth in

the corners of its mouth were as long as human fingers. She could smell the tiger's awful, meaty breath.

Ploo tried not to show how scared she was. Both of her hearts were beating three hundred beats per minute. She continued sending messages directly to the tiger's mind:

Little girls taste awful, Ploo esped. If you eat a little girl, you will have a terrible stomach ache.

The tiger roared. Then it stood up on its hind legs. It was ready to attack.

A man wearing a shiny white jumpsuit and a cape walked into the room. "Vat are you girls doing in zat cage?" shouted the man. He had a German accent. The front of his jumpsuit had sparkly letters on it that read SIGMUND.

"Get out of ze cage now!" screamed Sigmund.

Ploo Is Huge in Vegas

Looking down at Ploo was the biggest, scariest animal she had ever seen anywhere. It was even worse than the dreadful *shmerdlik* on planet Loogl. The huge tiger roared again. And that's when the morphing finally got going.

Ploo felt a tremendous itch in the middle of her back, right above her butt. Then a dinky little tail burst out of her skirt. Ploo's ears felt like they were going to pop.

They exploded into gigantic elephant ears!

The tiger seemed startled. It took a step backward on its hind legs.

"I said get out of zat cage!" Sigmund shouted.

It is working, Ploo! It is working! esped Klatu.

Ploo's nose drew in a gigantic gulp of air. Then it shot forward and grew as long as a stepladder. It turned gray and wrinkly and became an elephant's trunk!

You are doing it! esped Lek.

The tiger took another step backward.

On each side of Ploo's new trunk, two spots itched until they hurt. They burst open and two giant tusks shot out of them!

The tiger shut its mouth and dropped down to all four paws.

Ploo felt her body swell as though it were ready to burst. Suddenly her belly blew up like a beach ball. Ploo had become an elephant!

Hooray for Ploo! esped Lek.

I knew you could do it! esped Klatu.

The tiger turned around and trotted to the other side of the cage.

Elephant Ploo moved slowly forward. She was careful not to step on the little human girl. Ploo reached her trunk toward the little girl. She gently wrapped the trunk around the girl and lifted her off the ground.

The little girl shrieked with glee. "Higher!" she shouted.

Elephant Ploo swooped the little girl high into the air. She carried her to the door of the cage. Sigmund stepped forward and opened the cage door. Elephant Ploo gently handed the little human girl out to Sigmund.

"Sank you," said Sigmund. "Zat vas nice. But of course you know zat ve invented zis trick five years ago."

In a dark corner of the room, a man stood with a cell phone in his hand. He had seen Ploo morph into an elephant. His mouth was open in amazement.

"Boss, you're not going to believe what just happened," he said into his cell phone. "The little girl climbed into the tiger cage and turned into an elephant!"

"You're not making sense, Marcel," said Armand. "Have you been drinking?"

"No, of course not," said Marcel.

A few feet away from Marcel, Klatu realized he had a problem.

"Uh-oh," said Klatu. "My head just got bigger. I am starting to morph."

"My gum is . . . start to losing its flavor," said Lek. "We must to leave now or we are doomed!"

Lek and Klatu grabbed their money bags. Their heads and eyes were growing fast now. They were starting to lose their human shapes.

Come on, Ploo! Let us get out of here! esped Klatu, running for the door.

Ploo suddenly felt so tired she couldn't move. *Go on without me. I will catch up.* Ploo esped. She sat her six-hundred-pound elephant butt down on the floor of the cage. She laid her big, gray, wrinkly head down . . . and fell asleep.

"Uh-oh," said Marcel into the phone. "The old man and the kid are leaving, Boss. I gotta go."

Lek and Klatu left the hotel through the back door. Marcel raced after them, his feet crunching on the gravel path. He saw them run into the alley behind Circus Circus. He crept around the corner of the building and stopped.

Fifty feet ahead of him, something

weird was happening. It was so weird he thought he was dreaming. The old man and the boy were standing in the middle of the alley. They were leaning against a building. They were changing shape! *They weren't human!*

Marcel dialed his cell phone again. "Boss," he said, "this is Marcel. You're not going to believe what I'm seeing here!"

"Where are you now, Marcel?" asked Armand.

"In the alley behind Circus Circus. After the little girl changed into an elephant, the old guy and the boy ran back here. Boss, their heads suddenly got bigger! And, Boss, they have these long, buggy antennas growing right out of their heads!"

"Marcel," said Armand, "if this is a joke, it's not funny!"

"No, Boss, I swear!" said Marcel. "It's no joke! Everything I told you is true! It's happening right in front of me as I speak!"

"So what you're saying, Marcel," said Armand, "is that these people are turning into some kind of giant bugs?"

"Right, Boss!" said Marcel. "They're monsters! Hey, this could explain how they cheated at roulette!"

"Marcel, you've been drinking," said Armand. "Don't call me again until you've sobered up."

"No, Boss," said Marcel. "I haven't been drinking, I swear! Boss? Boss!"

His boss had hung up the phone.

6

Nowhere to Run, Nowhere to Hide

Did you hear that? esped Lek. *The humans know we are here!*

Who knows we are here? esped Klatu.

The human who is standing back there in the shadows. I just heard him tell someone that he saw us change into monsters! Now they will come and capture us! They will lock us up in tiny cages! I cannot stand being locked up in a tiny cage! We are finished, Klatu—finished, I tell you!

Get control of yourself, Lek! esped Klatu. *We must leave here!*

Klatu grabbed Lek's hand and the two bags of money. He pulled Lek with him as he ran down the alley. The bags felt even heavier than before. His legs felt heavy, too. Morphing back to alien form was tiring, but they had no time to rest now.

The alley ended on a busy street. Everywhere they looked, there were huge neon signs. Everywhere they looked, there were huge hotels. Hotels with shows going on in front. Waterfalls. Things on fire.

Crowds of people strolled along the street. They were looking at all the waterfalls and things on fire. Nobody seemed to notice the two aliens.

Marcel followed them out of the alley. He was talking to Armand on his cell phone as he walked.

"Okay, Boss, they're running up the street," said Marcel. "Yeah, they still look like alien monsters. No, Boss, I swear I'm not drinking."

Lek and Klatu ran down another alley. There were several garbage cans in the alley, and one of them had fallen over. Garbage that smelled like spoiled fish lay all around it. A door in one of the buildings along the alley opened. A man wearing red suspenders and a straw hat looked out and saw them.

"Well, *there* you are," said the man. He seemed annoyed. "You're twenty minutes late! But at least you're already in costume and you have your makeup on."

Marcel had slipped behind a garbage can.

The man shoved Lek and Klatu through the open door. They were in the back of a theater, looking at a red velvet curtain. Onstage behind the curtain were four human females wearing feathers and hundreds of sparkly things.

"Hurry," the man said to Klatu. "You're on now!"

"On what?" asked Klatu. But the man had shoved him onstage with the sparkly women.

The red velvet curtain went up. On the other side of the curtain were lots of people. They were sitting at little round tables in the dark, drinking and smoking, watching the stage.

Klatu looked out at the people and waved. "Yoo-hoo," he said to the people.

The people laughed.

"Stick to the script!" hissed one of the sparkly women.

"If it has glue," Klatu said to the woman, "then I stick."

The audience laughed some more. They thought this was part of the show. The sparkly women looked confused. Klatu made a funny face, and the audience roared with laughter. They loved Klatu. They began to clap.

Klatu didn't know why they were clapping. Maybe they were trying to kill bugs. He didn't want to get bitten by bugs. He clapped, too. The people laughed.

Klatu, come back here, you varna! esped Lek. *We must leave!*

But Klatu was in no hurry to leave. He liked it on the stage.

Two small people rushed into the theater. They were wearing costumes that looked very much like aliens.

"Sorry we're late!" said one of the fake aliens.

"I can't believe you started without us!" said the other fake alien.

"Ralph, is that *you*?" the man in the red suspenders asked the bigger fake alien.

"Of *course* it's me," said the bigger fake alien. "Who's that onstage?"

"I thought he was *you!*" said the man in the red suspenders. He turned toward Klatu. "Pssssttttt!" he hissed at Klatu. "Who are you?"

"Who *I* am?" asked Klatu. He bowed. "Klatu. Klatu from planet Loogl."

The people in the audience laughed.

"Get off that stage this minute!" hissed the man in the red suspenders.

"Getting off *what* stage *which* minute?" asked Klatu.

The red velvet curtain came down. The audience thought this was the end of the scene. They clapped wildly. Klatu clapped and looked for bugs.

Marcel ran in the door.

"Who are *you*?" asked the man in the red suspenders.

"Me?" said Marcel. "It doesn't matter." He ran out.

The man in the red suspenders raced out onto the stage. He looked angry. He grabbed for Klatu, but Klatu got away from him. The man in the red suspenders chased Klatu around the stage. So did the sparkly women, but Klatu was too fast for them.

The people in the fake alien suits ran onto the stage. They tried to catch Klatu, but Klatu was too fast for them, too.

Lek ran onstage. Klatu got away from him, too. The curtain went up again. The people in the audience screamed with laughter at what was happening onstage. Lek caught Klatu.

We are leaving here now, esped Lek.

The curtain came down. The audience clapped wildly. They wouldn't stop.

"Who the heck *are* you guys?" asked

the man in the red suspenders. He didn't seem angry anymore.

"We are nobody," said Klatu.

"Listen," said the man. "The audience really liked the show tonight. In fact, they liked it lots better than the regular one. Would you like to do this every night?"

"Charlie, what are you *saying*?" asked the bigger fake alien.

"You wanting I do this every night?" asked Klatu. He began to smile.

"Yes," said the man.

"No," said Lek. "He not want."

"Why I not want?" asked Klatu.

The bigger fake alien grabbed Klatu. "Hey, buddy, are you trying to steal my job?" he shouted. "Are you trying to take food out of my children's mouths?"

"No, no! *Please* keep food in children's mouths!" said Klatu.

"Mushy, chewed-up, stinky food from children's mouths, full of spit?" said Lek. "Pooeeyoo! Disgusting!"

"You're saying my kids are disgusting?" shouted the bigger fake alien. He swung a fist at Klatu. He missed Klatu, punched the wall behind him, and screamed.

"*Not* disgusting!" said Lek. He yanked Klatu away from the fake alien.

"Not disgusting!" said Klatu. "Stinky, chewed-up food full of spit is *yummy*!"

Lek pulled Klatu toward the door and into the alley.

"Come back here!" shouted the man in the red suspenders.

"Now you don't *want* our jobs?" asked the smaller fake alien. "Is there something *wrong* with our jobs? You think our jobs aren't *good* enough for you?"

Run, Klatu! Lek esped. *Run or we are doomed!*

Lek and Klatu raced down the alley. The fake aliens ran after them.

"I said come back here!" yelled the man in the red suspenders. He ran after them, puffing hard.

The fake aliens and the man in the red suspenders were catching up!

Help from the
Booger Boy

Back in JoJo's cage, elephant Ploo was napping when something weird happened. She burped and all the air whooshed out of her like air from a balloon. She was soon on the floor, flatter than a blueberry waffle. She tried to lift her flat head. Nope. She couldn't move at all.

This is what I get for breaking the rules, she thought. *For morphing into something bigger than me. For morphing without going back to my own shape first. How will I ever get out of here now? How will I ever find Lek and Klatu?*

Ploo had forgotten about the boy who told Lek that eating boogers made you die.

But he was in the room, too. He was staring at the flat elephant on the floor. So was Sigmund the magician.

"A flat elephant?" said Sigmund. "I *knew* zis vas a trick! I vill roll up zis trick and put it avay. Maybe someday ve can use it in our act."

Sigmund entered JoJo's cage and scratched the big white tiger behind the ears.

No, please, do not roll me up! Ploo esped. But Sigmund couldn't hear her.

Sigmund rolled up elephant Ploo like a window shade and tied a rope around her. He left the cage and stood Ploo up in a corner of the room. Then he went back to the casino.

The boy who believed that eating boogers made you die stared at rolled-up Ploo.

Hello! said a voice inside the booger boy's head. I am the rolled-up elephant standing in the corner! Help me!

"Why should I?" asked the booger boy.

Because I am not really an elephant, Ploo esped. I am a little girl!

"So?" said the booger boy. He didn't see why a rolled-up little girl needed help any more than a rolled-up elephant.

If you cut the rope and unroll me, Ploo esped, you can see me turn into a little girl.

"Big deal," said the booger boy. He saw little girls every day.

If you cut the rope and unroll me, Ploo esped, you can see me turn into a creature from another planet.

"Honest?" said the booger boy. This interested him. "An ugly one?"

Humans at Area 51 had called Ploo ugly, but they were wrong. Ploo knew she was beautiful. What if this boy only wanted to see an ugly alien? Should she say she was ugly just so he would help her? No, it wasn't worth it!

I am not ugly, **Ploo esped.** I have a nice big head, big beautiful black eyes, lovely gray skin, and a perfect wavy antenna in the middle of my head.

"Cool," said the booger boy. An alien was worth seeing, even if he had to work a little to see it. He walked over to the rolled-up elephant. He untied the rope. Elephant Ploo fell over on the floor and unrolled.

Ploo was still very tired. But she knew she had to get out of Circus Circus and find her brothers fast. She put all her strength into one last morph: 1 . . . 2 . . . 3 . . . morph!

Nothing happened. Ploo was still a flat elephant.

"Liar," said the booger boy. "You're no alien. I'm gonna roll you up again."

He bent down and started to roll her up again.

No, wait! Ploo esped. *I just need a little more time!*

"I'll count to ten, liar," said the booger boy. "One . . . two . . . three . . . four . . . six . . . seven . . . nine . . . thirteen . . . ten!"

The elephant shuddered. Then, with a little pop, it changed into a creature with a big head, big black eyes, gray skin, and a wavy antenna in the middle of its head.

"Cool!" said the booger boy.

Finally Finding
Jo-Jo

"Yeah, they're running down an alley, Boss," Marcel panted into his cell phone. "Two fake aliens are running after them, and a man in red suspenders. And, uh, me." Marcel stopped. He had a cramp from running. "I *am* telling you the truth, Boss. Two real aliens and two fake ones. Wait! Here comes another one! Make that *three* real aliens now!"

Ploo had caught up with her brothers.

Ploo! Lek esped. *I thought you were doomed!*

Ahead was a stone staircase leading downward. Klatu, Lek, and Ploo stumbled down the stone staircase. They pulled open a heavy iron door and tumbled into a huge darkened room. They slammed the iron door shut and locked it.

The fake aliens and the man in the red suspenders pounded on the door. The sound echoed in the dark room like thunder. They couldn't get in.

Klatu, Lek, and Ploo looked around. They had stumbled into a very large room with several cars. A garage.

In the back of the garage was a truck. Parts of its engine were spread out on the stone floor. Sticking out from underneath the truck was a long pair of legs.

"Yoo-hoo," said Klatu to the legs.

"Excuse," said Lek to the legs. He hoped the legs were attached to something. He hoped they weren't attached to a monster with a huge mouth filled with hundreds of sharp teeth.

"Are y'all talkin' to *me*?" asked the legs.

The legs rolled out from under the truck. They belonged to a human female with yellow hair. She was wearing a dirty blue jumpsuit. She was lying on some kind of rolling cart.

"Well, slap my mama!" she said. "Are y'all what I think you are?"

She stood up and took a good look at them. Klatu, Lek, and Ploo were amazed to see the name stitched on the woman's jumpsuit pocket.

"Jo-Jo!" they shrieked.

"You guys are from another planet!" said Jo-Jo.

"Planet Loogl," said Klatu proudly.

"What in tarnation are y'all doin' here?"

"We in tarnation were coming to Earth to do science project for school," said Lek. He wished his English gum still had some flavor left. "But turned out badly. Klatu crash our spaceship."

"Did not!" cried Klatu.

"Did so!" cried Lek.

"Did not!" cried Klatu.

"Did so!" cried Lek. "And we cannot to fix. If cannot fix, cannot ever go back home to Loogl."

"But Lily say Jo-Jo know how to fix spacecraft," said Ploo.

"Lily?" shrieked Jo-Jo. "Lily at the army base? Y'all know my Lily?"

"Yes," said Ploo. "They capture me, but Lily . . . help me to escape."

"Well, cut off my legs and call me Shorty!" said Jo-Jo. "How is my little gal?"

"Healthful," said Ploo.

"Good," said Jo-Jo. "I love that little gal like she was my own kin. And where in tarnation is this here spacecraft of yours?"

"In tarnation of desert," said Klatu.
"Near army base."

"Uh-oh," said Jo-Jo. A frown scrunched
up her forehead. "That could be a problem."

"What is problem?" asked Lek.

"Well, if the folks at the army base saw your spacecraft, they sure as heck dragged it away by now."

"Seeing spacecraft is not problem," said Lek. "*Not* seeing spacecraft is problem."

"What do you mean?" said Jo-Jo.

"He mean when we crash, I disappear spacecraft with hide-a-craft," said Ploo.

"Hide-a-craft?" said Jo-Jo. "Is that somethin' to make your spacecraft go *invisible*?" Ploo nodded. "Well, eat my lunch and call me hungry!" said Jo-Jo. "What I wouldn't give for one of *them* babies! Where is this hide-a-craft of yours? Can I see it?"

"When captured, I drop hide-a-craft in sand," said Ploo. "Maybe tiny bit hard to find now."

"So where is it exactly?" asked Jo-Jo.

"In desert," said Klatu.

"*Where* in the desert?" asked Jo-Jo.

Ploo, Lek, and Klatu looked at each other.

"Just somewhere in desert. Short ride from town of Groom Lake," said Klatu.

"Well, that's not as hard as lookin'

for a needle in a haystack," said Jo-Jo. "That's like lookin' for a needle in a whole *field* of haystacks."

"Lily say maybe you help us," said Ploo.

Lek wondered if Jo-Jo would help them.

Jo-Jo sighed and shook her head.

Sighing and shaking the head are not good signs in humans, esped Lek.

Helping us might be dangerous for her, esped Ploo.

She does not want to help us! esped Lek. *We are doomed!* He turned around three times for luck.

"Hey, any friend of Lily's is a friend of *mine,*" said Jo-Jo. "Okay, kids, we got some serious searchin' to do. If y'all aim to ever get off this planet, we better get started *now.*"

"Good! We getting started now!" said Ploo.

"Good! We getting started now!" said Lek.

"Good! We starting getted now!" said Klatu.

Turn the page for a passage from
the third exciting book in
the weird planet series!

No sooner had the car turned around than they got an unpleasant surprise. A huge black SUV had pulled up behind them and was blocking the road.

"Where did *that* come from?" said Ploo.

The driver got out of the giant car. He wore a black trench coat and over his mouth was a mustache that looked like a caterpillar.

"It is Marcel!" said Klatu.

"We are doomed!" cried Lek.

Marcel had been stalking them since they'd won bags of money in Las Vegas. The casino boss was sure the kids had been cheating. He had sent Marcel after them to prove it.

Jo-Jo made another U-turn, but it was too late. The soldiers had spotted the pink Cadillac. They surrounded both the Caddy and Marcel's car. A soldier came over to Jo-Jo's side of the car. He was wearing a helmet and mirrored sunglasses, even though it was night.

"This is a secured area, ma'am," said the soldier. "You people are trespassing."

"Secured area, my *foot*," said Jo-Jo. "It's just a stretch of empty desert, hon."

"It's a secured area *now*," said the soldier.

"Why?" said Jo-Jo. "Because of that spacecraft?"

"What spacecraft?" said the soldier. "I don't see any spacecraft. But I *would* like to see your driver's license."

Jo-Jo laughed in his face.

"What for?" she asked. "Are you gonna give me a traffic ticket?"

"No, ma'am," said the soldier. "I'm going to take you back to my commander at the base for questioning."

Judith Greenburg

About the Author

Dan Greenburg has written everything from books and magazine articles to advertisements, plays, and movie scripts. But his favorite work is writing for kids, and he's had otherworldly success with popular series such as The Zack Files. Dan lives with his wife, author J. C. Greenburg, and his son, Zack, in a house on the Hudson River, which they share with several cats.